HUMANITIES
HEALTH
BIOLOGY
Economics
SOCIOLOGY
CALCULUS
LITERATURE
Grammar
ANATOMY
PHYSICS
World History
ENGLISH
POETRY

Gage Bairos
November 18, 2001

Compliments of
The Proia Family

BEASTLY
Basil

by Tessa Krailing
illustrated by Mike Phillips

PICTURE WINDOW BOOKS
Minneapolis, Minnesota

Editor: Dodie Marie Miller
Page Production: Brandie Shoemaker
Art Director: Nathan Gassman
Associate Managing Editor: Christianne Jones

First American edition published in 2007 by
Picture Window Books
5115 Excelsior Boulevard
Suite 232
Minneapolis, MN 55416
877-845-8392
www.picturewindowbooks.com

Printed in the United States of America.

Library of Congress Cataloging-in-Publication Data
Krailing, Tessa, 1935-
Beastly Basil / by Tessa Krailing ; illustrated by Mike Phillips.
p. cm.— (Read-it! chapter books)
Summary: When Beastly Basil goes to summer camp he is afraid everyone
is going to find out his terrible secret, but instead he is shown what true
friendship really means.
ISBN-13: 978-1-4048-3113-1 (library binding)
ISBN-10: 1-4048-3113-4 (library binding)
[1. Monsters—Fiction. 2. Secrets—Fiction. 3. Camps—Fiction.
4. Friendship—Fiction.] I. Phillips, Mike, 1961-   , ill. II. Title.
PZ7.K85855Be 2006
[Fic]—dc22   2006027252

Table of Contents

Chapter One

Everyone agreed that Beastly Basil was a very handsome little monster. His teeth were yellow and pointed like a wolf's. His eyes gleamed, and he had purple spots all over his skin.

All of the other little monsters admired him.

"He's so good-looking!" sighed
Sickening Susan.

"Like a movie star," sighed
Boastful Bertha.

"I wish I looked like he does," said
Disgusting Denzil, who was Basil's
best friend.

But in spite of what everyone else thought, Beastly Basil was not happy.

In fact, Beastly Basil was worried. He had a shameful secret—a secret known only to himself and his parents. And now he was scared the other little monsters would find out.

The trouble started on Monday morning at school.

"I have some exciting news," said Dr. Grim, the principal. "This year, we're having summer camp at Whispering Woods. Please raise your hand if you would like to go."

With a shriek of delight, all of the little monsters put up their hands. That is, all except Beastly Basil.

"What's the matter, Baz?" asked Disgusting Denzil. "Don't you want to go?"

"I'm not sure," said Basil with caution. "It depends on the date."

Disgusting Denzil waved his arm at Dr. Grim. "Dr. Grim, when do we go to camp?"

"From July 25 to the 31," he said.

Basil frowned.
He did some quick
addition on his
fingers. Then he
shook his head.
"I can't go,"
he said.

"Why not?" asked Sickening Susan.

"Because I can't, that's why!"
snapped Basil.

The others stared at him. It wasn't
like Basil to be snappy. He was
usually so polite and good-tempered.

"But you have to go," said
Disgusting Denzil. "It won't be
the same without you."

"Just think about what you'll
be missing," said Boastful Bertha.
"Sleeping in a tent under the stars."

"Cooking over an open fire," said
Sickening Susan.

"Playing hide-and-seek with all
of us in Whispering Woods," said
Disgusting Denzil.

Beastly Basil sighed sadly. "It sounds like fun," he said.

"OK, that settles it!" Denzil said. He grabbed Basil's arm and waved it in the air. "Sir! Sir! Basil wants to go, too."

"Good," said Dr. Grim. "I will give you all a letter to take home to your parents."

Basil tried to look as pleased as everyone else about summer camp. But underneath, he was very, very worried.

What if the other kids found out his shameful secret? They might laugh at him. Worse, they might not want to be friends with him anymore. They might never speak to him again.

And all because ...

(This is Basil's shameful secret. Look away if you don't want to be shocked.)

Once a month, when the moon is full, he turns into a BOY!

Chapter Two

Basil's mother read the letter from Dr. Grim.

"Summer camp? That sounds like fun," she said as she passed the letter to Basil's father.

"I used to enjoy camping when I was a kid," said Dad. "Of course you can go, son."

"But I can't!" cried Basil. "I've already worked it out. On July 29 there will be a full moon."

"Oh, I see," said Mom. "You're afraid the others will find out?"

Basil nodded. He was nearly in tears. "Why does this have to happen to me?" he asked.

"Because Mad Mabel put a spell on you, that's why," said Dad. "We should never have asked her to be your godmother. She always did have a strange sense of humor."

"We'd ask her to undo the magic," said Mom, "but we don't know where she is."

Dad put his arm around Basil's shoulders. "Listen, son," he said. "You must not let this stop you from going to camp. Why should the others find out? After all, the spell lasts only from midnight until dawn. Everyone will be asleep."

"Your father is right," said Mom. "Go and enjoy yourself, Basil. Just be careful, that's all."

Basil was very confused. Half of him was scared about what might happen. The other half badly wanted to have fun at summer camp with his friends.

"All right," Basil said at last. "I'll go."

"Great!" said Disgusting Denzil, when Basil told him the news. "Let's ask if we can share a tent. You won't mind my snoring, will you?"

"Not a bit," said Basil.

To his surprise, Basil found he was beginning to look forward to summer camp. As time went on, Basil grew more and more excited. His mom even bought him a new backpack.

At last the great day arrived. Fifty little monsters, together with Dr. Grim and Miss Peabody, climbed onto the bus. They set off for Whispering Woods.

"I wonder if we'll see Spooky Sybil,"
said Sickening Susan. (Spooky Sybil
was a wise old monster who lived in
Whispering Woods.) "People say she's
really, really weird!"

"I don't care if we do," said Boastful
Bertha. "She doesn't scare *me*!"

As soon as they reached the
campsite, they put up their tents.

That night, they had a delicious
supper of squid soup and
fried cow pies.

Then they had a sing-along
around the campfire. They sang
all of their favorite monster songs,
including "Ten Green Vampires" and
"Ging Gang Ghoulie."

Basil was really, really glad
he had come.

But as the week went on, he began
to feel more and more nervous. And
when July 29 arrived, he felt too
scared to go to bed.

"Lovely full moon," said Denzil as
he crawled into the tent that night.

"Yes, it is," Basil agreed unhappily.

Basil zipped up his sleeping bag and closed his eyes. But he knew he would not sleep a single wink. He lay there, scared, waiting to change.

Chapter Three

Disgusting Denzil stirred in his sleep. Something had awakened him. It was a rustling noise.

Cautiously, he lifted his head. In the dim light he could just see Basil's shadowy figure leaving the tent.

Was he sleepwalking?

Denzil caught his breath. Sleepwalking was dangerous. Basil might fall into a hole or bump into a tree. He had to go after him.

Denzil crawled out of the tent and looked around. Luckily, the moon was bright so he could see.

But where was Basil? Ah, there he was.

Denzil followed Basil into the woods. The leaves shook in the breeze. They filled the night with their strange, rustling voices. "Watch out, Denzil," they warned. "Be careful."

Now he knew why they were called the Whispering Woods!

Suddenly, Basil groaned and fell to his knees. Denzil rushed forward to help him, but he got the most terrible shock.

Gone was Basil's long, shaggy hair. Instead, his hair was short, light, and very neat.

Gone were Basil's pointed yellow teeth. Instead, his teeth were white and even.

Gone were Basil's gleaming dark eyes. Instead, his eyes were bright blue.

Gone was his purple-spotted skin.

He looked horrible!

Denzil covered his eyes. He had seen pictures of ugly creatures like this. They were called "boys."

But he had thought they existed only in books. He had never expected to meet one in real life.

"Oh, Den!" cried Basil. "You should not have followed me. I knew you'd be shocked. But I can't help it. It happens every time there's a full moon."

"W-w-why?" Denzil stammered.

"My godmother, Mad Mabel, put a spell on me when I was a baby," said Basil. "It lasts from midnight until dawn. But my parents can't ask her to undo it because we don't know where she is."

Denzil felt sick with horror. But he saw the misery and pain in Basil's strange blue eyes, and he felt sorry for him.

"Why don't you ask Spooky Sybil to change the spell?" he asked. "She knows a lot about magic."

"OK. Let's go find her," said Basil nervously.

"Best to go while the spell is still on you," said Denzil. "Then she can see what the problem is."

Basil hesitated. "I'll go if you'll come with me," he said at last. "I'm too scared to go by myself."

"Oh, all right," said Denzil shakily.

Chapter Four

Spooky Sybil's hut was hidden deep among the trees. Smoke curled from a chimney, even though it was summertime. A green light shone in the window.

"Go on, Baz," said Disgusting Denzil. "Knock on the door."

Basil hesitated. "She might not be friendly," he said. "People say she is really weird. She might even put a worse spell on me."

"It's worth a try," said Denzil. "You don't want to be stuck with this problem for the rest of your life."

"No, I don't," agreed Basil. Nervously, he knocked on the door.

It opened almost at once. Spooky Sybil stood in the doorway.

Her wild green hair was sticking up all over her head. An owl sat on one shoulder, and a mouse sat on the other.

"Yes?" she said in a crabby voice.

Denzil said boldly, "My friend Basil needs your help. You see, every time there's a full moon, this happens to him." He pulled Basil forward into the light.

"Sssssss!" Spooky Sybil was clearly shocked. "This looks like Mad Mabel's work. Am I right?"

Basil nodded miserably and said, "Please, can you undo the spell?"

"Come inside," Spooky Sybil said, standing back to let them in.

A strange green glow filled the hut. Small animals scurried across the floor. They climbed up the table legs to munch on bread and pieces of cheese.

Spiders hung from the ceiling. A fox lay curled up on the bed.

Spooky Sybil glared at the monsters. "I don't see why I should help you," she said. "You young monsters make far too much noise and scare my animals."

"We don't do it on purpose," said Basil. He stroked the fox's head.

Spooky Sybil watched him. Then she said, "Oh, all right, then. Hold this."

She handed Basil a mirror and grumbled, "Don't look into it until I tell you to."

Basil nervously gripped the mirror. Spooky Sybil took several bottles off the shelf. She poured the contents into a jug.

Next, she added some powder from a jar and some dried leaves. Then she held the jug under the owl's beak and said, "Sneeze!"

The owl sneezed into the potion.

Spooky Sybil stirred the greenish-grayish liquid. She poured out a glass and handed it to Basil. "Drink it up—every drop," she ordered.

Basil screwed up his eyes and drank. Denzil held his breath.

At first, nothing seemed to happen.

Then, slowly, Basil started to turn bright green.

He grew brighter and brighter, until finally he disappeared inside a huge green bubble.

Denzil watched fearfully. Would he ever see his friend again?

The bubble burst. And there stood
Basil, just as handsome as he was
before. Denzil breathed a huge sigh
of relief.

"Now you can look in the mirror,"
said Spooky Sybil.

Basil looked in the mirror. He gasped with delight. "Oh, how can I thank you?" he asked Spooky Sybil.

"Just be kind to all animals, birds, and insects," she told him. "That's the only reward I ask. And remember—keep away from crazy old women named Mabel."

"I will," promised Basil.

Basil and Denzil returned to
the camp to find the lights blazing.
Everyone was running around in
circles. The little monsters raced up
to Basil and Denzil.

"Miss Peabody saw you were
missing and sounded the alarm,"
said Boastful Bertha.

"We thought you'd been kidnapped!" said Sickening Susan.

Basil and Denzil grinned at each other. "No, we weren't kidnapped," said Basil. "It was such a beautiful night we went for a walk."

"You're so brave!" sighed Susan.

All of the other little monsters looked at them with admiration.

"Basil! Denzil!" Dr. Grim and Miss Peabody came rushing up to them. "Where have you been?" they asked.

"They went for a walk," said Boastful Bertha.

"A walk? In the middle of the night?" Miss Peabody looked shocked. "We've been worried sick about you," she said.

"Sorry," muttered Basil and Denzil.

"All right, everyone, back to your tents," called Dr. Grim. "I think we've had enough excitement for one night."

Basil agreed. He'd had more than enough excitement. But now, thanks to Spooky Sybil, he was no longer afraid of the full moon.

The spell was undone. Never again would he be changed into that scary creature called a "boy." He couldn't wait to tell Mom and Dad!

Look for More *Read-it!* Chapter Books

Looking for a specific title? A complete list
of *Read-it!* Chapter Books is available on our Web site:
www.picturewindowbooks.com

3053800021418Z
Krailing, Tessa.

E
KRA

Beastly Basil

J.L. MULREADY SCHOOL
HUDSON, MA   01749